P9-CLV-606

Stanley's Party

Written by
Linda Bailey

Illustrated by
Bill Slavin

KIDS CAN PRESS

Stanley knew he wasn't supposed to sit on the couch.

But his people went out a lot. And they never came home before midnight. So one night Stanley began to wonder what would happen if he sat on the couch while they were gone. Just for a minute.

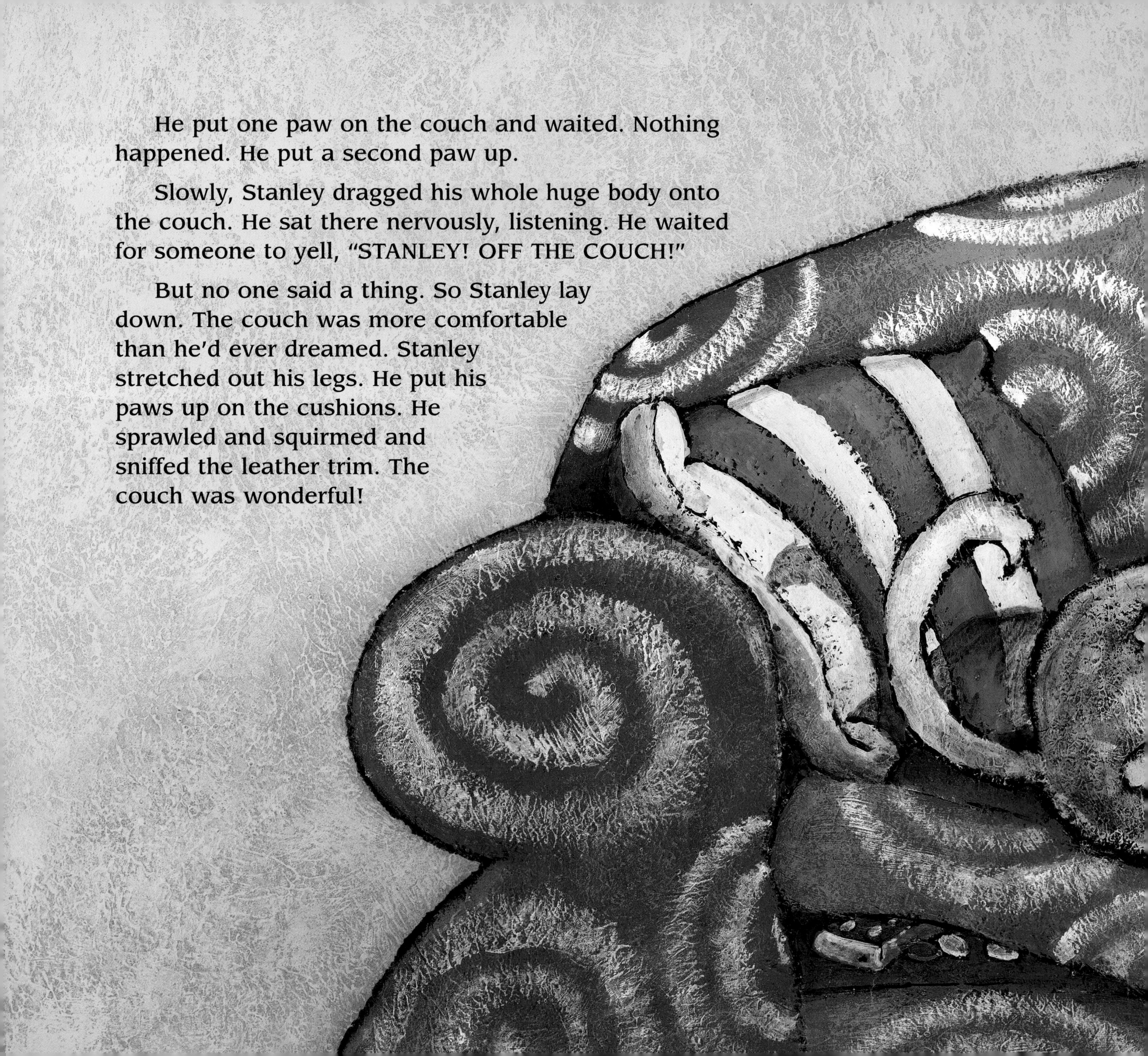

He put one paw on the couch and waited. Nothing happened. He put a second paw up.

Slowly, Stanley dragged his whole huge body onto the couch. He sat there nervously, listening. He waited for someone to yell, "STANLEY! OFF THE COUCH!"

But no one said a thing. So Stanley lay down. The couch was more comfortable than he'd ever dreamed. Stanley stretched out his legs. He put his paws up on the cushions. He sprawled and squirmed and sniffed the leather trim. The couch was wonderful!

All that evening, Stanley lolled and lounged on the couch. Just before midnight, he remembered his people. He straightened the cushions, brushed away dog hair, and hopped off the couch.

Whcn his pcoplc camc homc, hc was waiting at thc door. "Good dog, Stanley," they said.

"Rrrrff," said Stanley, wagging his tail.

Stanley felt terribly clever. He was so pleased with himself that the next night, he decided to try something new. He had noticed that when his people sat on the couch, they often listened to music. Stanley had seen how they got it.

He pushed some buttons with his nose. A moment later, music filled the room. Stanley was entranced! His body began to sway. His feet began to move.

Soon Stanley was waltzing around the room. When the music changed, he tried a cha-cha and a tango. He even did a bit of ballet.

Stanley danced up a storm that night. He didn't stop until just before midnight. Then he turned off the music and tidied the couch.

When his people came home, he was sitting on the living room floor. "Good dog, Stanley," they said.

"Bark-de-bark-bark," said Stanley.

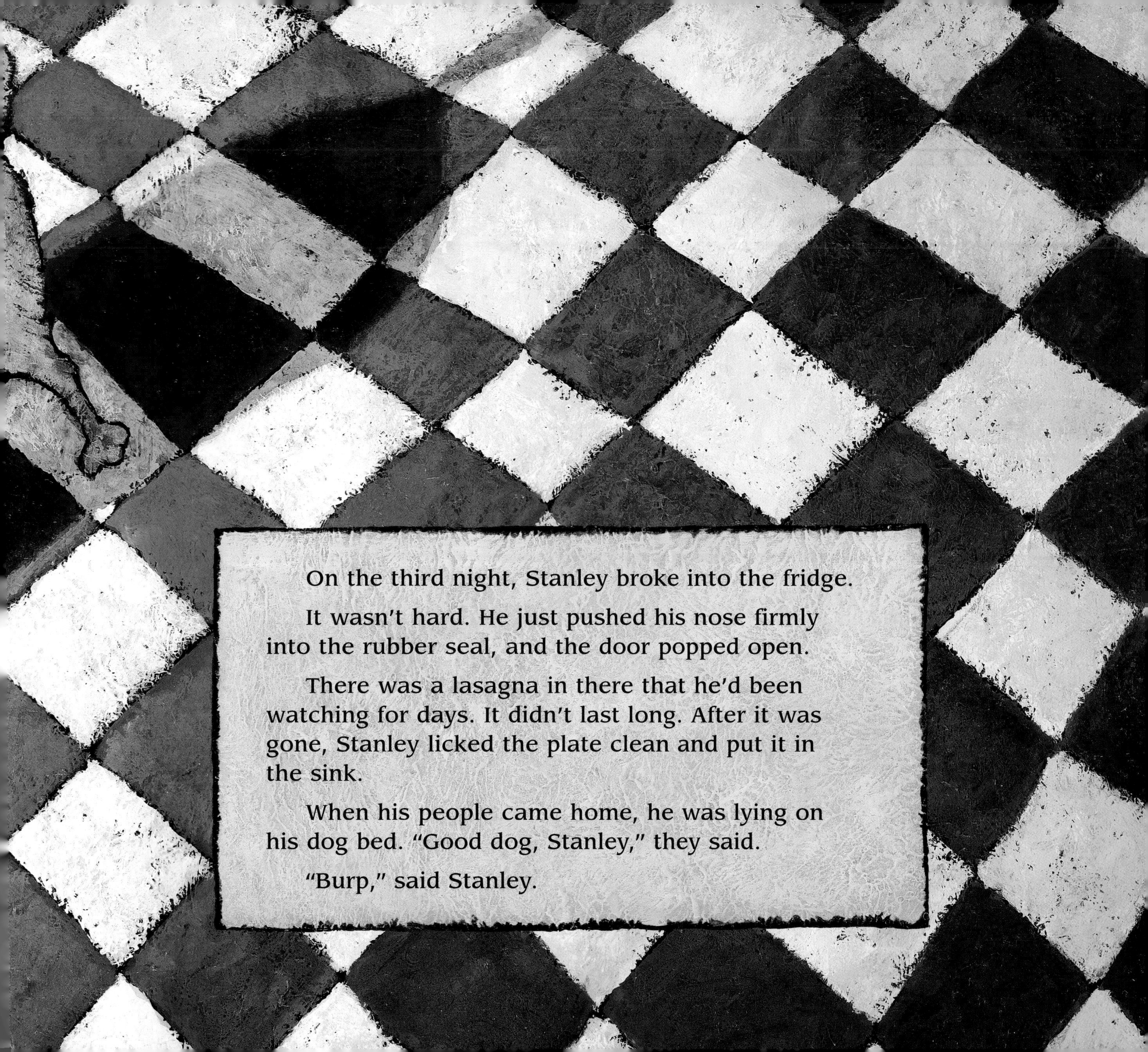

On the third night, Stanley broke into the fridge.

It wasn't hard. He just pushed his nose firmly into the rubber seal, and the door popped open.

There was a lasagna in there that he'd been watching for days. It didn't last long. After it was gone, Stanley licked the plate clean and put it in the sink.

When his people came home, he was lying on his dog bed. "Good dog, Stanley," they said.

"Burp," said Stanley.

Stanley couldn't believe his new life! Now he didn't mind at all when his people went out. As soon as they left, he sat on the couch. He sashayed and shimmied to the music. He nibbled and noshed from the fridge.

"I am having so much fun!" thought Stanley.

But after a couple of weeks, he realized that something was still missing.

And one day, when Stanley's people took him to the dog park, he figured it out. He was tired of having fun alone.

Stanley trotted over to his best friend, Alice.

"How'd you like to come over to my house this evening?" said Stanley in dog talk.

"What for?" asked Alice.

"We could sit around on the couch," said Stanley. "Put on some music, do a little dancing, maybe have a snack."

"Sounds great," said Alice.

“What sounds great?” asked Oscar, coming up to join them.

Before Stanley knew it, he had invited Oscar, too — and Mabel and Digger and Gassy Jack.

He invited two more dogs on the way home. And all the dogs he invited talked to other dogs, and those dogs talked to other dogs, and those dogs talked to still other dogs ...

That night, right after Stanley's people left, the dogs began to show up. At first they came in twos and threes. Then they arrived in packs. Some of them were Stanley's friends, but a lot more were strangers.

Stanley wasn't worried. "The more the merrier!" he said.

It wasn't long before the house was jammed with every kind of dog you can imagine. Shaggy dogs. Bald dogs. Dogs with wrinkles. Dogs with fleas. Humongous dogs. Weensy dogs. Dogs with floppy ears.

They filled the rooms. They packed the stairs. They flowed out onto the porch and lawn. Drooling dogs. Dainty dogs. Dogs that needed a bath.

"Anyone hungry?" asked Stanley, popping the fridge door open. Dogs poured into the kitchen.

"Help yourselves!" said Stanley.

Soon the fridge was bare.

"Anyone care for some music?" asked Stanley. He put on some rock and roll.

The dogs went wild! They stomped. They boogied. They bebopped and jived. They twisted and jitterbugged and mashed. They danced until their paws were sore. They danced till the whole house shook.

And who do you think danced hardest of all?

Stanley!

It was the best dog-gone party a dog ever had!

It was also the only night ever that Stanley's people came home early.

At first, they didn't say anything. Then they said together, very loud, "STANLEY! BAD DOG!"

All the dogs except Stanley had to go home. Stanley helped his people clean up. It took two whole days.

After that, whenever Stanley's people went out, they took Stanley with them. Stanley didn't mind. HE WENT OUT A LOT!

And he never came home before midnight.

As for the party, well, this all happened a long time ago. But in Stanley's neighborhood, the dogs still talk about that night. And the dogs that were there told other dogs, and those dogs told still other dogs ...

The story spread until dogs all over the country heard it. Then dogs all over the world. And now wherever dogs gather, from Turramurra to Timbuktu, they tell the story of Stanley's party ...

If you don't believe me, ask your dog.

For the members of the Vancouver Children's Literature Roundtable, especially Dr. Ron Jobe — a real party animal! — L.B.

For Joe and Murielle, who have a home where the dog party never stops — B.S.

Kids Can Press acknowledges the financial support of the Ontario Arts Council, the Canada Council for the Arts and the Government of Canada, through the BPIDP, for our publishing activity.

Published in Canada by
Kids Can Press Ltd.
29 Birch Avenue
Toronto, ON M4V 1E2

Published in the U.S. by
Kids Can Press Ltd.
2250 Military Road
Tonawanda, NY 14150

www.kidscanpress.com

The artwork in this book was rendered in acrylics, on gessoed paper.
The text is set in Leawood Medium.

Edited by Debbie Rogosin
Designed by Julia Naimska
Printed and bound in Hong Kong, China, by Book Art Inc., Toronto

The hardcover edition of this book is smyth sewn casebound.

CM 03 0 9 8 7 6 5 4 3 2 1

National Library of Canada Cataloguing in Publication Data

Bailey, Linda, 1948-

Stanley's party / written by Linda Bailey ; illustrated by Bill Slavin.

ISBN 1-55337-382-0

I. Slavin, Bill II. Title.

PS8553.A3644S73 2003 jC813'.54 C2002-902089-1

PZ7

Kids Can Press is a Corus™ Entertainment company